This book belongs to

A story for my little girl who is the fairy queen.

MARY THE HAIRY FAIRY

S. J. Vaughan

Mary the Fairy lived in a beautiful woodland, deep in the countryside, in a small fairy cottage with her parents, her six brothers and sisters, and her fairy cat, who was named Twinkle.

Mary was the youngest in her family and, although she tried very hard to be more grown-up like her brothers and sisters, everyone thought of her as the baby of the family.

 Mary's siblings all had very important fairy jobs. Her sisters Sparkle and Sugar Plum were flower fairies who made sure that all of the flowers were looking their blooming best at all times.

Her other sister, Airy Fairy, had a part-time job working for Father Christmas, making sure that all the girls and boys were behaving. She added their names to 'the list', before checking it twice and emailing it to the big man himself.

Mary's brothers were equally as busy and important. River and Star ran an agency, recruiting talented fairies for film and TV. They had even worked with Tinker Bell!

And Arthur, who enjoyed being a bit different, called himself 'Scary Fairy' and fronted a fairy rock band called The Nightmarey Fairies.

But Mary was the baby of the family – everybody told her so. She dreamed of following in her mother's footsteps and becoming a tooth fairy, travelling the world and rewarding children for keeping their teeth nice and clean. But there was one problem with this plan – Mary had a deep dark fear…

Mary's fear was so big and so scary that it sometimes made her feel like climbing into bed and hiding under the covers. Other fairies didn't understand it at all. You see, Mary had a fear of hairdressers!

You're laughing, aren't you?

That's ok. It is a bit odd. Everybody laughed at Mary and they would say things like, "How can you be scared of the hairdresser? That's ridiculous!" And they would call her names like 'Mary the Hairy Fairy'. Sometimes, words can be very unkind.

But the thing is, when somebody is scared of something, no matter what it is – spiders or ghosts or pink fluffy puppies – their fear is big and real, and Mary's fear was very big and very real. It followed her around like a tall dark monster.

The fear would tell her nonsense like, "If you get your hair cut, it will hurt so much your head will fall off," and "If you get your hair cut, it will NEVER grow back." And, every day, Mary would listen to her fear and every day her hair grew a little longer.

And every day her hair grew longer, Mary could see a little less.

Her hair was so long and so tangled that she couldn't see where she was going and she kept flying into things, usually trees and spider webs. This did not help Mary's hair situation. She had once flown through the serving hatch of an ice-cream van and ended up covered in ice-cream and sprinkles with a chocolate flake poking out of her hair! Poor Mary.

One morning, Mary's mother invited her on a gathering expedition to a nearby human village. Mary loved going into the village. She would hide behind flowers and watch the children playing in their gardens, and she would sit on rooftops and listen to their giggles while daydreaming about becoming a tooth fairy.

This particular morning, the sun was shining as Mary and her mother flew into the village. There was one house in particular that her mother loved to visit: a beautiful cottage with a garden full of flowers and a beehive where the bees would kindly share some of their delicious, sweet honey with the fairies.

Mary and her mother flew over the picketed fence and into the cottage garden. The sweet smell of roses and honeysuckle drifted on the warm breeze and Mary could hear the sound of a little girl's voice.

Being a very curious fairy, Mary flew off to investigate, while her mother went to collect some honey and other supplies from the garden.

The voice was coming from an open upstairs window, but, as Mary flapped her tiny wings and flew towards the sound, her tangled hair blew into her face and she flew off course, through the open window, bumping into the wall and landing on the windowsill with a splat.

A little girl looked up from her game. She wondered if a baby bird or perhaps a butterfly had flown through the open window, as they often do when you live in the countryside. But, to her amazement, as she got closer, she realised that it was not a bird or a butterfly, but a tiny little fairy.

The little girl was so excited! She had always wanted to meet a real-life fairy and she hoped that this one was alright after her unfortunate landing.

Very carefully, the little girl scooped Mary up in her hands. "Hello," she whispered. "Are you okay? You had quite a nasty bump."

Mary opened her eyes. She was a little dazed and she was sure she could see stars spinning around her head. She gasped when she saw the giant face staring down at her, and then she squealed when she remembered how humans were not supposed to ever see the fairies that lived all around them. 'I am in big trouble!' she thought to herself.

"It's okay," whispered the little girl. "You are quite safe. I won't hurt you." She sat Mary on her bed on a comfortable cushion. "I'm Evie," said the little girl. "What's your name?"

"I'm Mary," replied Mary, "but you are not supposed to have seen me. I'm going to be in so much trouble when my parents find out. If it wasn't for my silly hair blowing in my eyes, I would never have crash-landed."

"Well, I'm very pleased to meet you Mary," smiled Evie. Then she looked at Mary's hair with the tiny twigs poking out of it and the tangled bits of spider web.

"Do you want me to help you with your hair?" asked Evie. "I love playing hairdressers. It's what I want to be when I grow up." She waved a hand at the dolls she had been playing with. Each one of them had a beautiful hairstyle. There were plaits and bows, and there was long and short hair, pink and green hair and even rainbow-coloured hair.

Mary looked horrified! This was her biggest fear, right in front of her. A GIANT HAIRDRESSER WITH GIANT SCISSORS!

Evie saw the terrified look on Mary's face. "Whatever is the matter?" she asked.

Mary was shaking with fear and a tear ran down her cheek. "I'm ssssscared of hairdressers," she said and she burst into tears. "Everyone laughs at me. They call me Mary the Hairy Fairy, but I don't think it's very funny at all."

"You're right," said Evie. "That's not very funny and it's not very kind." She wiped a tiny tear from Mary's cheek with a tissue. "Maybe I could help you. I could just take the twigs out of your hair."

Mary nodded, though she was a little unsure.

Very gently, Evie pulled the tiny twigs from Mary's hair.

"That didn't hurt at all," said Mary in surprise.

"That's good," said Evie. "I can wash the cobwebs out for you if you would like me to?" She pointed to a small bowl of water that was on the windowsill.

Mary thought for a minute. She looked at the little bowl of water and Evie's smiling face. "Okay," she agreed.

Very carefully, Evie washed the fairy's hair. She used strawberry shampoo and conditioner – it did smell really good. She dried Mary's hair with a tiny towel.

"That feels much better," smiled Mary. She flew over to Evie's dolls' house and looked in the mirror. "It's still quite tangled, isn't it?" she said.

"Yes. I can brush it for you if you want me to," Evie offered. "I have small brushes, just right for little fairies."

Mary thought. "What if it hurts?" she asked.

"I'll brush your hair very slowly and carefully and, if it hurts, I promise I will stop," Evie reassured her new friend.

"Alright," said Mary, "we'll try."

Evie sat Mary on a little doll's chair on the windowsill and slowly brushed her hair. She started with the small tangles at the bottom before moving onto the bigger ones in the middle. Mary sat very still; she was quite enjoying having her hair brushed.

When it was done, she looked in the mirror and smiled. "That's amazing," she said. "Thank you, Evie."

"No problem," replied Evie. "I can trim it for you if you'd like, just to help it grow nicely and not get so tangled again." She picked up what seemed to Mary like a giant pair of scissors, the silver blades glistening in the sunlight. Mary was frozen with fear.

Evie picked up her new friend in her hands. "It's okay," she said. "It won't hurt one bit, and I won't cut it at all if you don't want me to."

Mary looked up at Evie's friendly, smiling face and suddenly she felt a little bit braver. "Let's do it!" she said. "I would like to have my hair cut."

"Brilliant!" said Evie. "Come and sit in the chair." Mary fluttered back to the chair on the windowsill. She felt a little nervous, but somehow Evie didn't seem like a very scary hairdresser. "You can watch all of the creatures in the garden and I will cut your hair for you."

Mary watched the birds and butterflies fluttering around the beautiful garden, while Evie trimmed her hair. It didn't take very long, with the scissors being so big and Mary being so small.

When she was finished, Evie used her toy hairdryer and a small comb to dry and style Mary's hair, before creating a beautiful plait complete with flowers. She held up the mirror so that Mary could see what she looked like.

"What do you think?" she asked Mary.

Staring at her reflection, Mary barely recognised herself. It had been a long time since Mary could see without her hair dangling in her eyes. "I love it!" she said. "Thank you so much, Evie."

"No problem. You are welcome to come back any time you need a haircut."

Mary smiled. Her fear had completely disappeared. It felt like a big dark cloud had lifted from her tiny shoulders. "I certainly will," she smiled.

Just then, she heard the voice of her mother calling. "Mary, it's time to go."

"I have to fly," said Mary, "but I will be back very soon."

"That's good," giggled Evie. "I have a really wobbly tooth and I'm in need of a good tooth fairy."

Mary nearly burst with excitement. "It would be my pleasure," she said.

"Mary, **come on**!" called her mother, who was struggling to fly with all of her shopping.

"See you soon," waved Mary, as she flew out of the window, without crashing, and off into the garden.

Mary's mother almost dropped her bag when she saw Mary with her hair so neat and tidy.

"Where have you been?" she asked in astonishment.

"To the hairdressers," beamed Mary. "I'm not scared any more. And now that I can see where I am going, I'd like to learn to be a tooth fairy just like you. Will you teach me please?"

Mary's mother almost cried. "I'd love to," she said, smiling, and she gave Mary a big 'proud mum' hug.

So, that's the story of Mary the (not so) Hairy Fairy. And, you never know, if you are sitting there with a wobbly tooth, Mary might be polishing a shiny coin at this very moment, ready to bring it to you...

Colouring Page

Colouring Page

Draw your very own fairy scene on these pages...

Printed in Great Britain
by Amazon